LÁSZLÓ KRASZNAHORKAI
Chasing Homer

LÁSZLÓ KRASZNAHORKAI

Chasing Homer

Good luck, and nothing else
Odysseus's Cave

with art by
MAX NEUMANN

with music by
SZILVESZTER MIKLÓS

translated from the Hungarian by
JOHN BATKI

A NEW DIRECTIONS BOOK

Originally published in Hungarian by Magvető as Mindig Homérosznak

Published by arrangement with the author and with Rogers, Coleridge & White, agents for László Krasznahorkai

PUBLISHER'S NOTE: Very special thanks are due to Ottilie Mulzet for her advice and invaluable help. Quotations from the Odyssey are based on the translation by George Herbert Palmer (1891).

Manufactured in China
First published as a New Directions Book in 2021
Design by József Pintér

Library of Congress Cataloging-in-Publication Data
Names: Krasznahorkai, László, author. | Neumann, Max, 1949– illustrator. | Miklós, Szilveszter, 1983– musician. | Batki, John, translator.
Title: Chasing Homer : good luck, and nothing else : Odysseus's cave/ László Krasznahorkai ; with art by Max Neumann ; with music by Szilveszter Miklós ; translated from the Hungarian by John Batki.
Other titles: Mindig Homérosznak. English
Description: New York : New Directions Publishing Corporation, 2021. | A New Directions book.
Identifiers: LCCN 2021022094 | ISBN 9780811227971 (cloth) | ISBN 9780811227988 (ebook)
Subjects: LCGFT: Novellas.
Classification: LCC PH3281.K8866 M5613 2021 | DDC 894/.51134—dc23
LC record available at https://lccn.loc.gov/2021022094

New Directions Books are published for James Laughlin
by New Directions Publishing Corporation
80 Eighth Avenue, New York 10011

Thanks to Aljosa and Petar Milatnak

Korčula, autumn 2016

You don't want to know.

Contents

Abstract

 Killers are on my trail, and not swans, of course not swans, I've no idea why I said swans—and not sheep, or doves, or a swarm of dragonflies—and I don't care, that's what jumped out, so that's what I keep saying to myself, *killers not swans*, something I keep on repeating because at times, rarely, but still, I find myself prone to lapses of attention, just for a moment or two, that's all, but for that moment or two my attention wanders, especially at times when I find a moment's rest on a bus stop bench, or mingle among tourists near some fountain, *killers*, I'll say, rousing myself, *not swans*, coming to my senses again, my vision sharp again, my hearing as keen as ever, meaning that I can sense with absolute certainty if they've gotten any closer, not as if I see or hear them, I've never seen or heard any of them, but my eyes and my ears are sharp again, and perhaps my nose as well, all my senses are still so vital to me, I have to know if they're getting any closer, after all I'm being hunted, they want to kill me, I have to keep this in mind, at all times, I can never afford to lull myself with any fleeting hopes that perhaps here— somewhere, sometime—I can relax, just because the acute danger seems momentarily to relent, no, the acute danger's omnipresent, and I have to remind myself that possibly they're waiting for just these relaxed instants, these moments of lapsed attention, although it's conceivable of course that their combat tactics, techniques of pursuit, and special hunting methods might perhaps be totally different from anything I can possibly imagine,

still, all the same, it could be that they're specifically targeting moments of weakness, yes, they might be aiming exclusively at my weak moments, perhaps that's all they want, to catch me at just such an instant, and the whole thing would be over, because of course they're out to get me and it's ridiculous to quibble over words, not only ridiculous but downright unacceptable to be splitting hairs here, it's cowardly, this kind of wordplay, it doesn't make any sense, when all along I'm perfectly aware that they're out to kill me, that's the long and the short of it, it's a game of patience, a deadly hunt they're conducting from a position of superiority, though it's also quite possible that they're actually set on making a cat and mouse game of it, they certainly have the requisite patience, they've been and still are ever so persistent, no, never for a minute do they seem exasperated, which would tell me that, yes, fine, up till now they've only been amusing themselves, but now enough of that, and at last they'll grab me, hang me, and gut me, disembowel me, decapitate me, cut my heart out, anything, just to finish me off, but no, in fact I never feel they have any impatience of that sort, but rather the exact opposite, though I know that they'll never relent, it's as if their orders aren't to make quick work of me, not to bring matters to a speedy conclusion, but rather to keep pursuing me forever, to never lose sight of me, and instead of focusing on the end result, the day when they'll finally have me in their claws and finish me off, they've been instructed to focus on making no mistakes, just keeping me in sight, shadowing me ceaselessly, staying on my trail so that I'll always be aware of what my life's like, nothing but a constant state of persecution until in the end this life, my life, will be ripped away from me—if they can catch me.

1. Velocity

It's quite obvious that it'd be a mistake to stick to a correctly chosen velocity, a mistake I can't afford to make even once, a fixed speed would make my movements predictable—the equivalent of my voluntarily, generously, spreading a red carpet before them, *this way, this way please, step this way and you'll be right on my heels*, no, that sort of thing won't do at all, and so, ever since this began I've been always opting for the wrong speed, making bad choices, but unpredictable ones, sometimes going too fast, sometimes too slow, and at times—my favorite method, if I may say such a thing—randomly alternating the fast and slow, to the point where such haphazard movements might almost call attention to me, but, no, there are limits, I can't become conspicuous, that would take away whatever crabbed enjoyment I can derive from all this, but in any case, there's no right speed for me, no correct choice of method, no segment of my flight where I can afford to make the *right decision*, the decisions I make must be the utterly wrong ones, always, without exception, that's how I can confound my pursuers, and similarly, in everything I do I must avoid all proper procedures, avoid any semblance of regularity, or reasonableness, or deliberate strategy—only chaotic movements, accidental decisions, only helter-skelter sudden, unexpected, unplanned moves that run counter to all logic can save me, so that's how I have to proceed, and that's why, once I'd realized that, yes, ever since, and after a lengthy, an

excruciatingly lengthy voyage, I'm once again setting foot on the coast, arriving at Pola, and getting swept forth in a crowd of passengers disembarking from the ship, yes, like flotsam carried by the waves, just catching a glimpse of the city's name on the giant iron sign posted above the dock, and yes, this is what I've been doing for decades, or at least for years, I've lost count of whether it's been decades, or years, but never mind what any rational calendar might indicate, maybe it's been merely months, or only weeks, I feel it's been years, possibly even decades that I've been on the road, but really what difference does it make if it's been only months, or just a few weeks, in fact I can even imagine that it's only moments ago that they handed down my sentence, its purport is perfectly clear to me, I haven't the slightest doubt that there's reason enough for the judgment, the only thing that's not yet clear is what that reason is.

2. Faces

 I believed for a long time that I really had to know who's on my trail, how else could I spot them, though I could only glance back, trying to catch one of them looking at me, yes, and I'd be trying to assemble their faces from glimpses, eye color, forehead height, a particular type of hairstyle, the shape of a nose, or of a mouth and lips, or the proportions of chin, eyebrows, cheekbones to an entire face, and so on, but whenever I assemble any such composite all I can see is just a uselessly ordinary face without any character or distinguishing mark, only a neutral, average everyday face, a face that says nothing, that could belong to anyone, and this led me down a perilously slippery slope, I'd start imagining that it's not just a few faces in the crowd, but the entire crowd's pursuing me, but then too I know this can't be true, because in any given throng, assembled for whatever reasons, in any so-called street crowd that I happen to find myself in, taking cover in it, it's clear that no one ever cares the tiniest bit if I'm there, nobody gives a shit whether I belong in that crowd, nothing interests a crowd, a crowd has no identity, no will, no aim, no direction, because no crowd ever realizes that it's a crowd, and so I've had to reorient myself regarding faces, I've given up trying to assemble my pursuers' faces from glimpses of foreheads, hair, noses, mouths, or ears, and instead I concentrate only on the look in their eyes, I read at a single glance the entire story of that look, whenever my eyes encounter

another pair of eyes when I whip around to see behind me, and by focusing on identifying the look in their eyes, I'm developing an ability I never possessed before, because in fact I must—by means of my own fleeting glance—perceive the entire history of someone else's fleeting glance, and for this, vision in any ordinary sense of the word isn't sufficient, since I'm forced to decide, via one lightning-quick backward glance, whether a certain look in someone's eyes, and its entire story, belong in fact to one of my pursuers—and I've been doing this all at a time when I'm not yet even sure how difficult it is, fully developing this ability, perhaps it isn't all that difficult—in any case, it's enough that I'm afraid, that I've been living in fear ever since I became aware that they're on my trail, in hot pursuit, and that my only chance of survival is to flee—and to keep on fleeing.

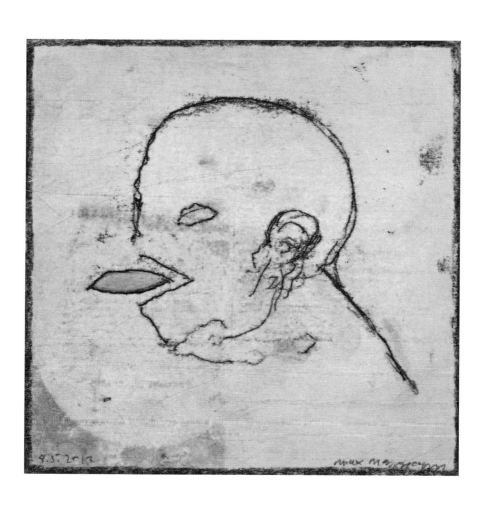

9.5.2017   max m....

3. Relating to sheltered places

I never received any training in the skills my life now depends on, my education was about different things entirely, I'd been taught Old High German and Ancient Persian and Latin and Hebrew, and then they'd instructed me in Mandarin and Japanese of the Heian era, as well as in Sanskrit, Pali and old Swahili, plus the language of the Csango people of Moldova, and then, of course without any warning that I'd in fact never need any of this, I'd been obliged to steep myself in Euripides and Xenophon, Plato and Aristotle, Lao Tzu and Confucius and the Buddha, while being required to read Tacitus, Cicero, Virgil and Horace, followed by Rumi, Dante, Shakespeare, Newton, Einstein and Tolstoy, and naturally then they'd hauled me over the coals of algebra, geometry, set theory, topology, discrete mathematics and analytical thought, nor did they neglect universal history, psychology, commercial bookkeeping (both local and international), anthropology, the history of science, philosophy and logic, and eventually I had to pass exams in the history of civil and criminal law, universal fashion history and even in the history of the Hungarian language, and all the while they neglected to provide me any particle of instruction in sawing and sewing, digging and hammering, welding, binding and dissolving, tying one thing to another and then untying them, my education had skipped all that—as well as survival strategies, unknown-terrain orientation, unarmed combat techniques,

not to mention defusing explosives, code-breaking, familiarity with spyware, protection against nuclear radiation, online systems' infiltration, much less any and all universal damage control or global preventive methods—and, now, when it's become obvious that my fate is to be on the roads, from one city to another, traveling by land and by sea, through deluge and drought, from zones torrid to freezing, day after day, hour after hour, from one minute to the next and moment by moment, well, I've had to learn everything from scratch, lightning quick, techniques must be acquired as fast as realizing that everything I need to learn isn't even real knowledge anyway, but really just a reflex, in fact it's all constant makeshifts, merely the sort of instinct you need to work a light switch: it's enough if you get good at flicking it on and off, to have the light instantly flash on or go out right away, and that's what's been happening, and in forming instant lightning-quick reflexes the most important thing is to understand that, in order to survive a lightning strike, one must not seek out sheltered places, for precisely such sheltered places are the most dangerous, since—in addition to the fact that my pursuers will naturally look for me first and foremost in such places—sheltered spots tend to increase your fear, the fear of unknown perils *outside*, a fear that simply regenerates and reinforces itself until it becomes overwhelming, making you incapable of drawing conclusions, or rather making you draw mistaken conclusions about *what's really taking place outside*, therefore these sheltered places are a suicidal strategy, one that eventually leaves you defenseless, so that the solution is precisely not to seek refuge in sheltered places but outside, and if anywhere, near the presence of danger itself, where there's a real chance to

ascertain and evaluate at first hand the actual reality of the peril and its immediate proximity, where instead of merely imagining what the level of danger from which I'm taking shelter *might be,* I can actually see or, more precisely, sense, that is to say correctly size up, whatever happens to be dangerous, where I can with unmistakable certainty identify the direction from which my assailants will ambush me, and so see immediately my escape route, for that's the only way to arrive at—of course within the fraction of a second—flight's technical details, that's the only way to pick the most suitable moment to escape and my best exit strategy, while—and it's absolutely vital to keep this in mind—remaining well aware that there's no such thing as *most suitable,* no such thing as *best,* and above all there's indeed no such thing as a way out, so that I, the fugitive, am forced to sojourn in precisely the very world from—and because of—which I'm fleeing. It's no use whatsoever to whine and complain that confronting danger intensifies the fear, which in turn could easily lead to making mistakes, so that—beyond the fact that in my view making a mistake, in a way, happens to be an important means of truly effective evasive flight in the most profound sense—soon enough, all the same I have to admit to myself and constantly must keep repeating the fact over and over again that not only am I forced to look danger in the eye, but I must downright seek it out, hunt it down and know where it lies, where the danger comes from to make plans right now to avert it; in sum, I have to persist, while realizing that my life isn't worth a hatful of crap, since it offers nothing other than (at a certain point of my flight, when my time comes) an inevitable failure: the collapse just before the end, self-denunciation, surrender, offering myself up—or, at best, just the end itself. A place of shelter will be ruled by terror and miscalculation, whereas out here in the open, I keep reminding myself even as I keep looking quickly over my shoulder, that that's out of the question, out here—facing forward again—it's just a state of constant, ceaseless, ever-present vigilance.

4. Relating to insanity

It goes without saying that the kind of life you're leading demands above all the most vigilant concentration, a type of focus that can never let up, can never remove its intent gaze from its object, never relax for an instant, but if there'd been time between two instants, it might have occurred to you that an existence concentrated in such a frantic manner, with your attention focused so exclusively upon a single point, carries the risk of, if not actually inviting, insanity as the result of such unbridled concentration, such focus upon a single point, and since the subject of the pursuit (namely you) can never know whether you're transgressing the borderline beyond which the life you're leading could be declared insane, when you might become uncertain and begin to doubt the reality of your surroundings, question the truth of having been on the run for years, possibly decades, certainly for months, weeks, days, hours, minutes, or moments now, and you might ask if this persecution is taking place in reality, or somewhere else, you might ask if you're indeed, as they say, *one of us*, one who, to all appearances is here, present, and in this shape fleeing from your assassins, or if you're merely a phantasm, a fabrication brought into existence by a totally different kind of insanity, perhaps a madness brought on by an excess of leisure … yes, you might think this over, after all there's something not very credible about a being—again as they say, one of us—living out your life in this sort of existence, imprisoned by decades

and moments, until you're finally caught and hacked to pieces, stabbed in the heart, garroted from behind with a wire, or quite simply have your guts literally trampled out by heavy boots, you might be aware that all of this could merit serious consideration, were there enough time for such considerations between two instants, but there isn't any, because there's nothing between two instants, because from one instant to the next, such a focused state of being remains uninterrupted, nonstop, ongoing, it's not even worth speaking of instants, especially not of *two* instants, moreover two *successive* instants, how ridiculous, and so your relation to your own insanity is best characterized by a perpetual ambiguity, wherein you yourself, as well as your insanity, exist in a permanent, billowing state of potentiality, exactly as you yourself, willingly bearing it and embodying it, do question it, because your insanity has not yet emerged from its haziness, well, in a word, you say to yourself, to make it brief, insanity is a question suspended in limbo, the answer to which must exist, but it would be like a mute person saying something to a deaf person.

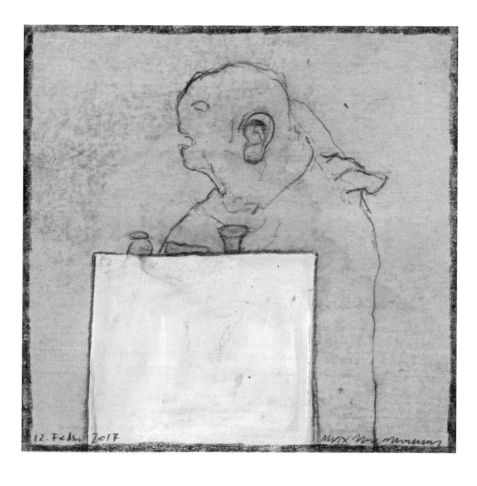

12. Febr. 2017   Max Neumann

5. Moving about in crowds

 You always have to seek out crowds, places where many people congregate, and you have to do this inconspicuously, without being noticed, in order to, how shall we say, integrate, blending in as if you've been there all along, and that's what I do, what I have to keep on doing, which doesn't necessarily mean, as soon as I spot a multitude at some new station, mindlessly rushing into its midst, and yet somehow I need to act along these lines, I have to keep on blending in at all times, to be not yet in the throng one moment, while in the next instant somehow already an integral part of that multitude, one among the many, moving along with the others, but constantly keeping in mind that you're in a crowd, a perilous place, too, and therefore you must be constantly aware, as in a swirling whirlpool, of the crowd's inner structure, where it's denser and where its weave is looser, always letting yourself be swept off in any direction, and if it thickens, be aware when it's sucking you in, and be mindful when it's pushing you out, or pulling you in, always being swept along, carried along to some neutral area, and blending in there without seeming to exert any effort, in other words always mindful, ceaselessly following this method, whether you happen to be on a street or at a port, or observing the tourist herds flocked together to see the sights of a given locale, or on a train, or aboard a ship, or standing in line for food, or at a water fountain, staying always, always, always within the crowd, sensing from the slightest vibra-

tions of its structure when to shift your place, and that's about all there is relating to crowds, just this, but always in exactly this way—that's how to exist in a crowd.

6. Advisory

But I'm in no position to be giving advice, and I've no time for that, though if I did have the time for such things, then I'd add, for example, about falling asleep that one should never sleep while on the run—I can't tell you how it's done, but do not fall asleep, do not shut your eyes for a moment, not even to blink, because all would be lost, and not so much because in that moment they could immediately pounce on you, for they can pounce on you at any moment, this doesn't depend on your eyelids, but because falling asleep is evidence of your fallibility, your unsuitability for escape—you might as well just give up right away, anyone who falls asleep while on the run shouldn't even think of trying to escape, since, after all, letting your eyes close on the run is like that first sip of whiskey to an alcoholic, that proverbial "just this one, and that's it," a person like that shouldn't even think about escape, to hell with it, give yourself up, the sooner you get it over with the better—just look at that deer, that little shit, it's time you realize that she's not the gentle little Bambi of children's stories, that's ridiculous, no, this actual little fawn hates everyone—perhaps on account of that fairy tale, impossible to find out exactly why—but the point is that this hypocritical beast, to tell you the truth, bites, but that's not why I brought her up, that this little shit bites, but because when you chase her, she won't take the trouble to escape but instead, thinks better of it, and after a few leaps and bounds, lies low to wait and see if

she will squeak by, well, that's you if you're going to fall asleep on the run, this whole thing isn't for you, better leave it to people like me, for, among other things, I do not fall asleep, I don't know how I do it, but I don't sleep, I wouldn't be able to sleep, I'm a creature incapable of sleeping, though at times I have to keep saying this to myself when my body all of a sudden craves sleep, as it sometimes does, there's no denying that, nor am I denying it now, but it's the vehemence of my self-reprimands that always enables me to evade these moments of crisis, and which will keep saving me, even when my head first nods forward, and then my little eyelashes wink shut—but no, no, I do not fall asleep, I'm incapable of that, I really am, and of course the vehemence of my self-reprimands helps, but what really keeps me awake is the thought of the pleasure my murderers would feel finishing me off if they realize that it can be done while I'm sleeping.

But there's more.

Actually, you're not supposed to eat, either. Or drink. I'll explain it—yes, I am speaking to myself, as always, as if I'm speaking to someone, even though I never speak to anyone, only to myself, carrying on my permanent dialogue with myself, not a dialogue that can survive me, although, yes, I admit—naturally I nibble on something every once in a while—of course I gulp down a few swigs from time to time, but this can't qualify as eating and drinking, because my watchfulness at these times, on these occasions, is if possible even more intense, so that I can barely swallow, in fact eating as well as drinking is a torment, chiefly because while you'd think that this watchfulness, this straining to sense if my murderers

11.5.2017   Max Neumann

are approaching with frightening speed behind my back as I'm eating or drinking, could not in fact be elevated to an intensity greater than it is at the times when I'm not eating or drinking, yet the intensity *does* elevate, that's to say it's impossible, it causes such excruciating agony that even to think of eating or drinking makes my throat go into such spasms that I no longer want to eat or drink, though naturally that doesn't mean that I won't eat or drink again, even though it should, but in any case, I especially do not advise *you* to try it, because this is not for you, you might as well keep on stuffing yourself, and just let whatever has to happen, happen.

But even that's not all of it.

Let me explain.

You must keep everything that's good far away from yourself. And there are so many things that are good! Yes, it's ever so good to be in the midst of that moist warmth! So good to be in your mother's lap! So good in a thicket of mown weeds, so good between a gutter's slimy stones! And the impossible is good! And the unconscious is good! And the forbidden is good! It's so good to feel your blood pumping! So good to plunge into the surf, and so good, for once in your life, to blindly and mindlessly run backward at full tilt! And so good to bite into rubber, into tar or raw meat! And so good to stand on your head and stay there! And so good to roll down a slope carpeted by fragrant grass! So good to dip into anything as soft as the body! And so good to fuck, oh boy, to fuck away and all the while not knowing why! And even the bad is good! And the good's also good . . . !

EVERYTHING'S GOOD!

But I don't want everything, I don't want anything, I have no need for any of these good things, for if I ever even *think* of these good things, it'll surely be curtains, they'll nail me, if they haven't already nailed me, just as they'll eventually nail you, if you hope to escape your murderers but you can't say no to anything good: the good is the most insidious trap of all.

I must explain this, once and for all.

The good isn't a moral category, the good is that deceptive condition that makes you easily recognizable, simplifying you and rendering you defenseless, for the good lulls you and dulls you, persuades you that if you're in the good, then you're in that eternal space, for being in the good suggests that you have nothing more to do, there's nothing else to be done, now you can relax, stretch, crack your knuckles and kick back, for when you're in the good, time comes to a stop, the good takes you outside of time, as if a mother materialized to take you out of school, and there's no more cramping up with schoolwork tension or taking exams tomorrow, cowering at a desk in a classroom dreading that the teacher might call on you, being in the good deludes you into believing that the chase is over for you, and that you may now calmly stroll down by the riverside, find a nice quiet spot to cast your newest Korda Kaptor lure, and the sun's shining or the rain's drizzling, and the grass is growing around you, you can actually hear it growing, but you don't participate in it, you're not part of the universal rush to grow, to swell, to be rosy, to ripen, to mature, to age, to grow facial hair if you're a woman, or a slack, ponderous pair of testicles if you're a man, where nothing and nobody can disturb you now, you imagine, when you're in the good, though the most dangerous thing in fact is that you're no longer taking any cognizance of your pursuers, and even if you do think of them, they get lost in a mist, positioned there in the good you cannot identify your murderers, their characteristics simply vanish, it's impossible to guess their shape and form, their nature, their vulnerability or invulnerability, to the point where I can't even decide what's more terrifying, the unknowability of my murderers, or everything that is good.

7. Adapting to the terrain

 I can't afford to abstain from speaking to people, but whenever I'm forced to speak, it must be in the most cautious manner possible. I must avoid giving replies that are obvious platitudes, and at the same time everything I say must be neutral, yet still in accordance with expectations, suited to local customs, in a word, as natural as the breeze or the rain or a tavern opening its doors because it is ten (or nine, or six) in the morning. I need phrases that say something while saying nothing at the same time, phrases that keep problems away, the problems of answering any questions about me, for that's the riskiest subject, when I'm obliged to say a bit more about myself, while saying precious little, much less anything about what I'm actually up to, and all this within a territory smaller than, say, from Pola here down along the coastline for a short distance, to Fiume, say, or to Abbazia, my statements must of necessity be free of any contradictions, that is they must relate to each other more or less harmoniously, after all I can't claim in Pola that I came from Scotland, and then state in Fiume or Abbazia that I arrived from Norway, I must remain consistent, and nowhere may I withdraw or act completely aloof, no, true to my tactics, in addition to being part of a crowd at times, I must occasionally also be able to fit into smaller ensembles that may form around me, for instance on a park bench or while eating—in my case an extremely brief meal—or at a drinking fountain, if my timing's so poor that while

I'm drinking—once again, just a few gulps, that's all!—
somebody steps up and stands behind me, waiting in
line, because then I can't just rush off, I must allow a bit
of time for the other person to say something, in case
he has something to say, to which I'm then obliged to
make the most neutral reply possible that still suits the
occasion, for instance if that person remarks *we're having a real scorcher today, it must be tough for you with
that gimpy leg*, well then, I can't just turn around and
leave without saying a word, but must provide a reply
of the sort that's least likely to invite the other to make
a rejoinder, therefore I have to say something merely
to the tune of *you said it, man, it sure isn't easy*, and
that's all, not a word about the whys and wherefores,
and not a word about what's wrong with my leg, that
because of a knee and thigh injury in early childhood
I've always had a slight limp, not a word about that,
just let the last drop of water trickle from the vicinity
of my mouth before nicely slipping aside without being
too quick or too eager about it, making sure to linger
a moment or two while the other takes up his position
by the water fountain, and leaving only when the other
person, clearly about to finish drinking, might be contemplating an inquiry about that injured leg, well then,
that's when you move on, that's how you do it, and indeed that's how I act every single time, so that I simply
never do anything to call attention to myself, no one notices my existence, so much so that if someone were to
inquire whether anybody has seen me, most probably
everyone who'd chanced to cross my path would reply
in the negative. Naturally I'd be in trouble if say, on one
occasion—just once—for some reason I did feel like an-
swering when asked where I've come from, because I

myself don't know where I've come from, since I have no memories whatever, thanks to the fact that nothing that I've left behind possesses the least significance, the past doesn't exist for me, only what's current exists, I'm a prisoner of the instant, and I rush into this instant, an instant that has no continuation, just as it has no earlier version, and I have to tell myself—if I had the time to think about this between two instants—that I have no need for either past or future because neither one exists.

But in fact, I have no time between two instants.

Since there's no such thing as two Instants.

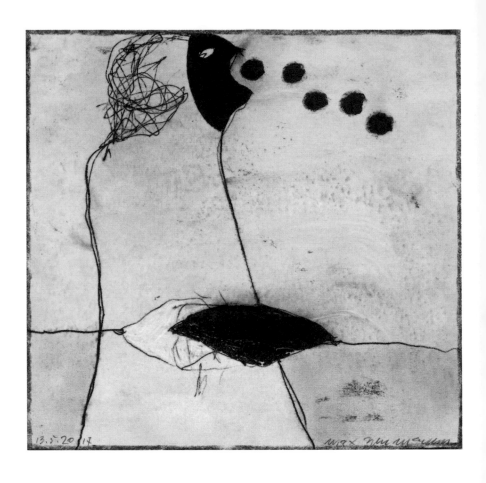

13.5.20 14   max neumann

8. On the meaning of pursuit & murder

It's impossible to decide whether they're hired assassins pure and simple, or else aficionados of the hunt, killers driven by a passion for the game, I never dare to really think through either possibility, but given a choice, I'll opt for killers out for the sake of the hunt, and what scares me the most is the possibility that they really have no feelings about any of this, not now, when they're on my track, nor when they at last corner and surrounded me, and proceed to beat me to death with the bludgeons they carry, this persistence of theirs, the way that they're becoming, at the same time as me myself, ever more resolute, I know this phenomenon well—it mirrors practically exactly what I experienced when I realized that my flight would last more than just a few days, that it would last for weeks, possibly months, years, decades, but in spite of all that, I don't like drawing such parallels, since they could easily lead to the misconception that, seen from the vantage point of that nonexistent Highest Dispensation, their pursuit and my flight are merely two ways of looking at the same process, and such a hypothesis would be distasteful, in fact downright repulsive, so, no, I conclude that my flight in no way mirrors my killers' actions, there's no equivalence at all, such logic is unjustifiable, and implying some connection is a line of reasoning containing something deeply, atrociously immoral, immoral in the sense of speaking of killer and victim in the same breath, as if the one could not exist

without the other, and that's why, I realized in Zara one night, I detest mathematics and would banish it from the world, mathematics together with everything else that has the least connection with mathematics, because mathematics makes no allowance for—and, what's more, doesn't even acknowledge—the universality, the actual reality of moral questions, it merely allows that morality has its place, but not here, not among us, it has no place here—to hell with your morality: our equations and formulas and analyses and extrapolations, our axioms and the framework of our entire mode of thinking exclude the possibility of allowing for such matters— in fact the most horrendous of all assertions made by mathematics is already present in the simplest addition— that one plus one equals two—I can't possibly imagine anything more repulsive, even the mere thought of this sort of addition fills me with nausea, because then I'd have had to concede that all this is independent of anything: what this one would be, and what the other one would be, not to mention two, their so-called sum; I'd have to concede that all this is independent, one might say, free of all other things, detached as is everything that reeks behind any mathematical expression of this sort, no matter how much more complex, while being resplendent at the same time, in consequence of which I realized that the way matters stand with me is that I've never defined my own flight in terms of what it means that they're after my life, that I have to run for my life is a perfectly closed, separate world, as is the world of those who pursue me, if you can call it a world, the existence of such desperadoes as the ones who are after me, in other words I ultimately must say that while my flight does have a purpose, for my pursuers I myself am

not their aim, but their mere given, a sheer by-product, a *waste*, so it makes no difference whether they're hired assassins or passionate hunters. Yes, their sheer *waste*.

9. Life

 I never feel that my life is something that is mine, something that belongs to me, that it's a den nobody else can enter, where nobody can see in, as if a curtain's been drawn, but the truth is that I've never thought about what my life's like, I didn't even know where something that's my life is supposed to be located, I see the lives of others, but that's no actual life either, others do not possess lives any more than I do, something that belongs only to them, that nobody, as it were, could take away from them, surely no such thing exists, and if someone were to ask me, *so tell us, please, go ahead and tell us what you really think*, I'd reply, a life?—there's no such thing as a life at all, because people who bandy this word about take it for granted that this word *life* has a meaning, an ultimate meaning even, though we may not know what this ultimate meaning is, in the old days it had been thought of as one thing, and we think differently today, but it is absolutely certain, these people say, that life does have an ultimate meaning, and they are satisfied that with this utterly unacceptable statement, or exclamation, which at times they slam a hand down on the tabletop to reinforce, they have settled the entire matter, but no, the matter has not been settled at all, although I won't make the absurd claim that the word *meaning* signifies nothing, it does have a signification, but does it make any sense?! Are you joking? And it is the same with life, it too has only a signification, but does it make any sense?! Let's not kid ourselves! And

then we can take the next step, because it is the same thing with having a purpose, again it's the same unpardonable, irresponsible exaggeration, leading moreover to a massive, irreversible misunderstanding, for nothing has an *ultimate* purpose, because nothing has any purpose, it is always just one particle of existence that is itself nothing but a process, wandering from process to process, or more exactly, tumbling from one process to another, to thrash about until tumbling into the next process, so that instead of a purpose it has a consequence, and what they—mistakenly! mistakenly!—call purpose is the result of the raging of particles carried along by processes determined by chance, but it's nothing except mere consequence, that the particle, the process, must constantly suffer, and that this suffering—more precisely: this enduring—is life itself, and therefore life as a whole possesses nothing whatsoever, only its inner processes offer something, namely the way life resurrects like a spark and immediately expires amid the delirious war of consequences, without anything ultimate or any similar inanity, life is forever merely the incalculable consequence facing the oncoming process, because there's nothing that lurks behind the process, that is, no consequence points toward the past, nor is there one that indicates the consequence that will follow after the next one, there's only the coercive force of consequences driving any given moment, not so that another moment should follow, naturally, for there is no other, none at all; I myself am unable to distinguish a stone from a brook, a brook from a trout, not to mention that from time to time these trout leap from the water, so how can I be expected to be able to assert that life ... no, no, and anyway I'm not very handy with words that denote general

15. 5. 2017   max neumann

concepts, for me nothing exists that goes beyond the situation that happens to be at hand, I don't really have time to think about these things, and mainly no desire to do so, because I dislike, no, I *despise* questions, for after all, and this cannot be repeated enough, I despise answers as well, the only thing that exists for me is the spontaneous, the unpremeditated, the bewildering act and its concomitant terror, and the wherefore of getting away, that's all there is, to be quicker than those who are after me in order to douse me with gasoline in revenge for the length of time it took them to capture me, grinning as they bring the lighter's flame very slowly closer and closer to my body, so that I could say, under duress, that when you stand there paralyzed and stinking, doused with gasoline, and see the flame of that lighter getting closer and closer, and when you still just manage to feel yourself being slightly lifted by the propulsive force of the explosion, only to have your small body spatter into tiny fragments before it's consumed, go ahead and try querying then about such things as: what is life.

10. Choosing an escape route

 If you think, if you consider, then you're doomed, I think, pondering about not thinking, about not pondering, about which direction I'm least expected to take when I take off, they could imagine, for all I care, that I'm heading homeward, it makes no difference what anyone thinks about this, the only thing that matters is the *how*, since I'm forced to rely solely on sudden and fortuitous decisions that are completely unpremeditated, a sudden departure without any past, present, or future rationale, and so all of a sudden I take off, and now I'm scurrying, I'm getting away from them as best I can, because I can sense that they're on my trail, and not just on my trail, but, and this is far, far more horrifying to realize, they're not only pursuing me, but out to murder me, and at a time like this you can't afford to think (I'm thinking later), there's no room for deliberation, and not only because, especially not because there's no time, but because, with a start that seems incomprehensible and illogical to them, I can confound the reasoning that goes on in my pursuers in such cases, assassins like that are always following a plan, assassins like that are always consistent, and assume, taking it for granted, that the person they have to kill goes this way or that for one reason or another, but when he goes this way or that for no reason at all, the killers don't know how to handle that, and after all, when this horrible chase began, it came in handy that I didn't know what I was doing, and so it follows that, if I were to devise a plan of

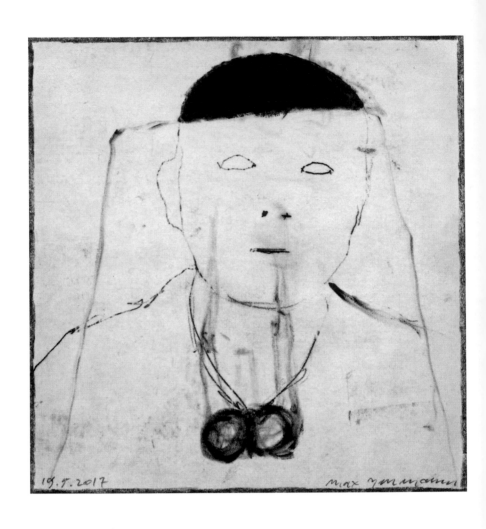

19.5.2017   max neumann

some kind, it would be all over for me, for no matter what the plan might be, it would have to be rational, it would be either a good or a bad decision to go this way or that, hide here or over there, except that I began my flight mindlessly, and this must have been why I've succeeded in getting this far, when of course I couldn't have known, and in fact don't know, just how far I can proceed with this, but I am paying no mind to the future: as a matter of fact I simply don't give a shit about the future, it holds nothing promising for me, chiefly because it doesn't exist for me, only the moment in which I find myself exists, which leads us into the stinking infinite, both me, the hunted one, and those who mean to seize me in order to first rough me up a bit and then inflict every imaginable torment upon me, for taking so much time to surrender, until in the end they do what could have been done right at the outset, they'll wring my neck, break it, snap my head to one side, unhinging my vertebrae, and it's done.

11. Stations

I've no idea what country this is, as far as I'm concerned it could be any country, I've quickly picked up the most important words of the language, enough to patch together the simplest sentences, so that's no problem, I have no trouble buying bread at the store, or returning empty bottles to get the small change for their deposit, this goes fine, the language, I've quickly assembled the few sentences and phrases I need, and although I've formed no idea whatever of the country, that does not interest me, where I am at the moment, I just very quickly realize what's doable and what's not, which way is possible and which isn't, that this is Pola, and there lies Rovinj, and Rovinj is to be avoided at all costs, sudden notions such as these come to me completely by happenstance, for after all why couldn't I have gone to Rovinj, I later ask myself, well, just because, no reason at all, it's a question to be shooed away, because it's a dumb question, and I hate dumb questions, just as in general I dislike all questions, as was mentioned earlier or will be, later, I'm not sure, at times one or two questions do crop up, but I try my best to avoid them, I have a poor relationship to questions, they just make me nervous, because they don't lead anywhere, and where could they lead me, when I have no need for answers either, so this is how it goes, not toward Rovinj, I'm already on my way in the opposite direction down along the coast, merely making sure I keep close to the coast, near the sea, for me the sea and land are

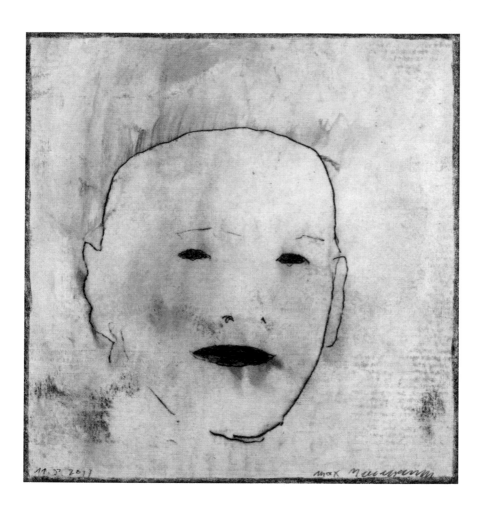

11.5. 2011   max neumann

the two great immediate possibilities, and so Abbazia
becomes my destination, Abbazia and points beyond,
and so I spend a lot of time nosing about in ports, around
ships, many a time I stand in the waiting crowd, watch-
ing some local ferry or giant cruise ship fill with people
and then slowly float away outward bound, but for the
time being I'm not embarking on any of them, not yet, for
now I'm hugging the shoreline, winding my way southward, always toward the south, for the time being this
is my route, but no buses, never by bus, whereas I take
trains frequently, but only local trains, they have just
the right number of passengers, and I'm not confined to
a tight space, as I would be on a bus, and I can survey
the scene at a glance, a passing glance can take in the
layout of the station, which travelers board which train
car, I can scan their faces, their luggage, their jackets
or umbrellas, whatever, allowing my passing glance to
decide whether I should get on that train at all, or immediately leave and look for a southward way by some
other means, why exactly south I can't say, and it really
doesn't matter, it could have been north just as well, or
west, but in spite of it all I'm opting for the south, and
that's that, I'm holding myself to that decision, although
not because I believe that it's the safest way, no direction is safer, but because I don't want, by deciding "suddenly north" or "suddenly west," to imply that I possess
some agenda, in which case heading south would be in
fact not a very good choice, although it's not a poor one
either, after all it makes no difference, so south it is, the
main thing is that insisting on this direction seems to
make no sense, and therefore I insist on it, thinking that
this will continue to bewilder the kind of brains I imagine inside my assassins' skulls, so that yes, I keep on

advancing along the coastline, believing—while of course I can't have the least assurance that this is how it would be if I keep on this course—that eventually this direction will come to an end, I'll come upon a cliff that drops off straight down to the sea, and that will be the end of the road, somehow I imagine it like that, standing there aghast where the cliff drops off straight down to the sea, and that will be the end of the south, and then one can either start climbing, or else turn back, there's just one thing I mustn't do, and that's to stop and stare at the cliff dropping off down to the sea, because if I get stuck there staring out, then in a hot second they'll be there and seize me, break my lame leg, crush my hands, rip my head apart by tearing open my jaws, no, I won't stop there, that's for sure, to gawk at the cliff dropping away down to the water, where the south comes abruptly to an end.

12. Value of earlier observations

The mouse is a very stupid creature, I can't imagine why I'm thinking about this at such a time, but no matter, at times this thought comes to mind, and at such times I get into a bilious mood, I can't in the least understand what scientists want with these mice in their research labs, really now, it's utterly ridiculous that they assume a creature such as the mouse has intelligence, a mouse has no brains, whatever it has is a mere rudiment, a promise of a potentiality never realized, take a sober look at the mouse, especially a white mouse, gallivanting about in a laboratory where it's been placed by scientists so that it should kindly demonstrate how clever it can be, well, it isn't clever, it's stupid, as dumb as a post, plus on top of that totally spoiled, eating and drinking until it's bloated, life as a luxury cruise, all it has to do is occasionally run around in the maze where the researchers place it, that's all, and it runs headfirst into a wall, it hasn't the brains to see in time there is a wall ahead, no brains at all, but enough of this, let's drop it, it makes me so angry that I'll say no more, just this, that mice are dumb, and hateful, that's all, I'll waste no more words on the matter, because a brain as obtuse and useless as a mouse's is not even a brain really, a mouse has no brain, a mouse just is, and exists solely for the purpose of showing off under artificial lights in those specially constructed labyrinths, which are, how shall we say, incredibly simple to take in at a single glance, the mouse is simply repulsive, and not even a real beast, if you think about it, and in the

15.5.2017   Max mecke dein.

end they put that piece of cheese in there and lean over to observe with satisfaction how, after considerable difficulty, and with some luck, one of these indolent, fat little hunks of meat at long last stumbles upon it and starts to nibble, the blood rushes to my head, but truly, each and every time I think of mice, although I have nothing to do with them, absolutely nothing, why, I have more affinity with, with a, with a bat than with a mouse, I simply detest mice, may they rot in hell, on one occasion I saw a mouse in a laboratory, and it still makes me furious, just thinking about it, there it was, basking in the light from above, reluctant to set out after the cheese—they kept nudging it, let's go, there's that nice bit of cheese, not interested? nope, it wasn't interested in the cheese, it just about lay down on its back, paws under its head, legs crossed, that's how comfy and cozy it felt, sunbathing, but seriously, enough about mice, there's nothing but nothing to be learned from the mouse, it's no use to claim otherwise, if you take the trouble to watch it carefully in that labyrinth, but let that really be enough now, I'll stop now, I really can't understand myself why I feel such an onrush of rage on account of a mouse, I'll choose some other object to detest, there are so many detestable things, such as wild bats, for instance, but for me it's the mouse that really gets my goat, I'm the first to admit it, nothing else can enrage me as much as this wretched little critter, and let that really suffice for now, how can I afford to think about mice when there are murderers on my trail, and I must plunge, from the edge of a moment right into its midst, and onward, from one wave to the next, just like some Moby-Dick, or a dying butterfly between two flower petals, I must keep fleeing, even if on top of everything, as I may have already mentioned, there's no such thing as two moments.

13. Faith

 A person in so stressed a situation prefers either to avoid the question, or to confess that he's a believer, because, that's the way it is, at the ultimate hour, when one must confront death, everyone, as they say, becomes a believer, whatever else they might claim is a lie, yes, there's even that joke about how the number of atheists decreases in an airplane about to crash as the ground rushes up, very funny, ha ha, and I have to shake my head, standing just at that moment in the port of Split waiting for a ship along with other travelers, or more precisely pretending to be waiting since I don't have the least intention of embarking just now, I'm merely obeying a sudden impulse to mingle in the crowd, to gain a bit of time until it becomes clear where to head next, in short, I'm standing here, reflecting whether, if I'm not a believer, I can still believe in fate, including my own, being directed by some Higher Power, but no, I don't believe in that at all, I've never felt the presence of a Higher Power, and, given my situation, I simply can't afford to start believing just out of fear, since after all it's completely certain alas that there are no Gods, no Higher Power, because *only what is right here* exists, no, no *belief*, that isn't for me, although prayer's quite another matter, there's always a need for prayer, yes indeed, invoking Zeus and Athena and all of the Gods in Heaven, Thetis, or Triton, or Amphitrite herself, Anyone or Anything, to save me yet again, one more time, just this once is all I'm asking for, I'll never ask again,

just this once to be saved by Zeus in the Sky, Athena in the Heavens, or Aeolus himself, or Whoever or Whatever in Distant Space, I'll promise anything, I'll do anything, I'll promise not only to be a believer, but to be a great believer, who will never have doubts, never say such things as I did just now—that belief isn't for me, and only what's right here exists, things like that—and not only would I not say such things, I won't even think them, I'll perform the sacrifices, again and again, I'll perform them every month, and chant the sacred words along with the priest, and partake in the holy rites, I will chant along with the *aulos*, and pronounce the ultimate last words with arms uplifted to the sky, if only right now the Lord or Whichever God upon the Peak of the Mountain of Mountains would save me, I am well aware that this sounds strange coming out of my mouth, I who have pronounced so many phlegmatic sentences all my life about how and why I'm unable to believe, how very truly sorry I am, but what can I do, I see through the nature of belief and therefore am utterly unable to follow its path, not that I'm inclined to do so, yes, I have to admit that's just how it's always been, but now, from this sacred moment onward, I won't be like that, and lo, I'm not, not anymore, for I now believe with my entire being that Zeus in the Sky will succor me, so I will be humble, and I'll never indulge now in a single debate about faith, never again will I argue about belief, joy will flood my heart for not taking part in debates about faith, for I am a believer now, and a believer can never take part in any controversy fueled by erroneous and arrogant notions, and anyway, I'll now give arrogance a wide berth, realizing that this selfsame arrogance, scorn, and lack of humility have led me to this impasse—when I'd believed in nothing, especially not in the Immortals, or in the bastards engendered by Immortals, or in the myriads of little beings of one sort and another—yes, this was actually what I'd come to, such exclamations and arguments—but today I'm beyond all that, nowadays I pray frequently, even now I'm praying in the midst of these travelers here at Gate 2 in Split, I'm pressing my hands together just above my lap, in the penumbra of my body so that nobody can see, and I bow my head and pray, trying the prayer so pleasing to Athena, that's the one that comes easiest, and when I don't know the words I make them up and keep on going, racing to the final lines, and I'm concentrating so energetically on advancing by means of this prayer that when I get to "You Are the One" I'm saying it aloud, not too loud, but some of those around me hear it, though pronounced in a language incomprehensible to them, and, although they don't give me any looks, when I'm done a middle-aged lady, with an old-fashioned boa around her neck and with her abundant blonde hair piled up high in a gigantic bun, turns to me to say, and not in an overly friendly tone, rather in a somewhat ... dutiful manner: No need to worry, according to the weather forecast the Bora, which will turn out to be more like a Borino this time, is still quite a ways off.

13. Mai 2017   max neumann

14. Korčula

 Well, I ended up boarding that ship at Split, forced to do so unexpectedly—my perambulations up and down along the piers had made me sleepy, and sleep overcame me while walking, until all of a sudden I jerked awake, feeling that they'd caught up with me and were almost laying hands on me, but I came to my senses and raced away from the spot—never again, never can I afford to have this sort of thing happen again, such a lapse of attention, and actually this has never happened before, their getting *this* close, though I couldn't see their faces this time either, but then I've never actually caught a glimpse of them, all I've ever had was merely a constant awareness of their presence, which has been enough to avoid being nabbed by them, always enough, and anyway there really isn't any need for me to see them, I have no desire to see them, scared that the sight would make me so afraid that I won't have enough strength left, because seeing them would paralyze my will to escape, but not this time—I was already stepping up onto the gangplank propped against the side of the ship, because this is the most unexpected thing I could do, to embark and disappear together with the ship, a choice I'm entrusting, as always, to chance, but I only travel as far as Dubrovnik, as far as the money I got for returning the bottles could take me, and there I disembark, and I wander around for a couple of days among all the other loiterers, but it doesn't feel right in Dubrovnik, so I say no to Dubrovnik, refusing Dubrovnik, and once again

I'm looking for a ship, but not because a water journey seems safer than going by land, but, as always up till now, *just because*, just because this is how things happen to be shaping up, as I follow in the wake of a pair of feet, a pair of feet in petite red shoes, keeping my eyes only on those feet, stepping exactly where they step, which is why I find myself on a new ship, this particular one, where those feet led me, but now this means, yes, taking on that additional, perhaps unnecessary risk, namely that I neglected to buy a ticket, nor do I have enough kunas for it, and although my brilliant scurrying technique, mastered long ago, enables me to get aboard without being caught by the purser checking tickets, nonetheless I don't dare to remain on deck like this and so I seek a cranny, some safer place to hide in, until I can disembark, and after going this way and that I find a narrow little doorway leading down to the darkness and earsplitting racket of the ship's hold, where the roar of the engines obliterates all other sounds, I'd traveled like this before, in the vicinity of the engine room, and had not liked it, just as I don't like it now, I hate this brutal, enormous power thumping and thundering—inflating and deflating, shaking and rattling, this indefatigable death rattle—these ships' engines know only one tune, a merciless music written to the score of *no-can-do-no-can-do-no-can-do*, yes, every one of these engines is like that, they're dying from the word go, getting ready for that right from the beginning, when they were installed in the hold of the ship, and keep on dying until the end of time, I'm always afraid of them, and I'm afraid now, although I don't have much of a choice, I have to put up with it, of course I'll take shelter here among the thick, hot pipes, though if anyone were to glimpse me down here, I'd be easy prey, yes, and on top of it all, I'm

the only one to blame for following that pair of little red shoes that enticed me here, where I really don't want to be, but I have to stay now, trusting myself to these engines, and trying to guess from their painful bellows where the ship's going—are we still out in the open sea or are we nearing some coast, where the port's name might be Bari or something like that—but no, that's not what's happening, and when it grows dark outside, I can sense that the dreadful engines are changing register and are easing up somewhat, so I creep up on deck for the first time, as the ship's coming to anchor on an island, the name of which I can't make out because from my vantage point the sign with the place's name is completely obscured by a eucalyptus tree, but then I can't stand not knowing where I am, I insist on seeing the sign at any cost, and it's safe to say that's my sole reason for disembarking on the island, and I do read the sign, after which, since I don't dare remain alone in the harbor with its buoys, I quickly fall in with the few passengers getting off the ship, all locals, returning home from work or from school; the island, especially now in the gently descending twilight, appears to be tranquil, and although I don't like tranquil places where I never know if I've arrived at one of those so-called sheltered zones which are off-limits for me, but in spite of this and in any case, as I soon realize, I'm already off the ship for good, because—while I hesitate, at a loss about what to do next, getting swept a little ways alongside the others disembarking—the sailor's already pulling up the gangplank and slipping his ropes from the buoys, all the while keeping an eye on me, so that it seems wiser to stay with the group of homebound locals, and go on in the direction most of them are taking, across a piazza, where they each go their own separate way, without a word, not even a goodbye, as if—every day the same boat at the same time—they've seen each other enough times over the past years or decades not to be standing on any ceremony, in fact I think people around here, along the Adriatic coast, are not terribly friendly anyway, as if all of them have lived through too much here, which might have something to do with the Bora, that evil cold wind, which is perhaps invoked too often in these parts, as if the Bora, with its bad reputation, had cursed them with such a morose temperament, and around here even the reckoning of time depends on whether an event occurs before the Bora or after (neither option apparently very heartening), so I detach myself from the scattering home-ward bound troop and stop to look back at the wake of the departing ship as night descends, while the locals rapidly disappear into one narrow alley or another, leaving me alone out here, except for the moon, which peeks out from among fleeing clouds, suddenly casting its clear light on the town just when I need it to get my bearings, since I don't remain still for long but start to roam about, this way and that, and soon I've covered the entire little town which has grown silent and utterly desolate, the only sound the ship's foghorn in the distance, while here in the narrow alleys the houses have shut themselves up so thoroughly that not even the clatter of dishes can be heard, unless it's the local custom to prepare the dinner plate for the one coming home without making the slightest sound? and as I pass the securely iron-grilled windows I'm think-ing, is it possible? or could it be that the extreme exhaus-tion of my endless flight is deceiving me?—but I feel the growing sense that those who've been persecuting me for decades—or at least for years, months, weeks—had not been on the ship and are therefore not present now.

15. Mljet

Yes, soon after midnight the Bora arrives, and by dawn I'm frozen to the marrow, not only my head and hands but my whole body's shaking by the time the first bar opens on the harbor that hugs the island's southeast corner, where morose-faced men and women materialize, leaning against the counter and drinking watered wine, raising a glass for a swallow, then putting it down in front of them, all the while saying not a word, without even glancing at each other; if anyone, it's the bartender they're eyeing, with whom they'll exchange a few words, but of course I don't understand a word they say, so that it's a diversion when—as the heated room gradually brings my shivering to an end—a tall, gray-haired old man with an air of authority enters, a local tourist guide, it soon turns out when, speaking a well-modulated English saturated with the usual strong Croatian accent, he ushers into the bar an elderly Japanese couple who seem somewhat reticent or embarrassed (waving to the tourist guide from the outside, indicating that they don't want to come in), but he's determined—if not overly friendly—and with a rather exaggerated cheerfulness he, already indoors, keeps gesticulating and expostulating, citing one reason after another, insisting they should not hesitate but come on in, after all, the open door's letting in the cold air, while all he says to the bartender is, "the Bora," nodding toward the outdoors, this might be a greeting, for the bartender, a young, very thin blonde girl replies, in a low

mumble, *da, stigla je,* as the new arrivals seat themselves at a table that happens to be near mine, where I
sit with my hands around my warm mug of coffee, and
overhear the old man asking the Japanese couple what
they'd like to drink, whereupon after lengthy discussion
they ask for cappuccinos, and the guide steps over to the
counter, places the order, and now I notice that the man's
limping—if ever so slightly—on one leg, while the Japanese couple, who, judging by their clothes and behavior,
have obviously traveled here for touristic reasons, launch
into a heated argument, in low voices, in their own language, only falling silent when their cappuccinos arrive,
and that's when the old tourist guide starts in, *look here
now, it's really worth seeing, a wondrous nature preserve,* he's not saying this because it's his livelihood, no,
he's been retired for some years now, only his wife works
part-time a few hours a week at the landing stage, whenever the ferries (which had formerly belonged to her fam-
ily) arrive or depart, but as for him, he's no longer
working, so it isn't a matter of his having any business
interest in this, but he'd still like to convince them, *at
least hear me out,* he says, cutting off the timid protests
of the couple seated facing him, who are clearly signal-
ing that they do not wish to see something that's not to
be missed, and the tourist guide goes on in his proficient
English, *look here,* he says leaning closer to the couple,
*you should realize that this happens to be the ultimate
experience for any tourist who bothers to come all the
way here,* and he isn't saying that Korčula isn't worth it,
Korčula *is* worth it, Korčula is beautiful and full of precious historical sites, not to mention that Korčula is close
to his heart, after all he's a native of this island, he's lived
here all his life, and this is where, when his time comes,

he will die—Korčula is like a part of his body, *but the truly top attraction is not here, my dear lady*, he says, now turning to the woman, in the hope that she'll prove more receptive, or less likely to resist, *the real attraction lies over there*, and he nods in a vague direction, *during the season tons of small boats go there*, he says, *but this time of year hardly any, but of course a way could be found*, and it wouldn't be any trouble for him to get them on a boat leaving whenever they want and returning at a prearranged time, in other words, it's doable, and he can only repeat that this is not in his own interest, *it's for your benefit*, pointing at them as at two culprits, whereupon they clutch their cups even tighter, *if you miss seeing this brilliant site, this matchless wildlife preserve that's simultaneously a memorable spot in world history, why*, the tourist guide went on, *that would be the equivalent of traveling to Rome and not seeing the Sistine Chapel, do you understand?!* he exclaims looking at them, piqued that they need so much persuading, and he takes a swallow from his mug, then pulls a book out of his pocket, opens it to the first page, and begins to read, still in English, *Tell of the storm-tossed man, O Muse, who wandered long after he sacked the sacred citadel of Troy* ... and here he winks at the Japanese couple, *longing for his home and wife, the potent nymph Calypso*, and looking at them again, raising his voice menacingly, he repeats, *the potent nymph Calypso*, you see, *a heavenly goddess, held in her hollow grotto, desiring him to be her husband* ... then, seeing that the two of them don't appear to be wholly convinced, he shuts the book, raises it with his right hand and shakes it a bit in their direction, as if he intends to convey to them without using words, that, *look here now, this is Homer, it's not me speaking, but Homer himself, understand what I'm saying?* then he opens the book again and hemming and hawing begins to leaf through it, and after a good deal of leafing his index finger suddenly comes smack down upon a line, and he recites, *when he reached the distant island,* and pronouncing those last two words, *distant island,* he once again winks at the couple, who this time make no effort to hide their bewilderment, or the fact that they'd very much like to leave now, because they don't in the least understand what's going on with this book and with this recital, but he goes on, *there turning landward from the dark blue sea, he walked,* and here we are talking about Hermes, he explains, *until he came to a great grotto where dwelt the fair-haired nymph,* and here he interrupts the reading for a third time, as his index finger now marks the place where he left off, and he merely repeats, significantly, with a beseeching grimace (as if saying, there, you heard it? do you get it?!), *dwelt the fair-haired nymph,* and he raises his hand, waving it rhythmically as he reads on, reciting, *Upon the hearth a great fire blazed, and far along the island the fragrance of cleft cedar and of sandalwood sent perfume as they burned. Indoors, and singing with sweet voice, she tended her loom and wove with golden shuttle. Around the grotto, trees grew luxuriantly, alder and poplar and sweet-scented cypress, where long-winged birds had nests—owls, hawks, and sea-crows ready-tongued, that ply their business in the waters. Here too was trained over the hollow grotto a thrifty vine, luxuriant with clusters; and four springs in a row were running with clear water, making their way from one another here and there. On every side soft meadows of violet and parsley bloomed, and so on, and so on,* the old man hums, hmm, hmm, his finger following the lines down the page, again looking for something, and when he finds it, his voice rings out, and he raises his index finger high, intoning, *at a glance Calypso, the heavenly goddess, failed not to know it was he; for not unknown to one another are immortal gods, although they have their dwellings far apart. But sturdy Odysseus*—do you hear what the poet is saying? he asks his victims who'd been attempting to rise by barely perceptible degrees from their seat on the other side of the table but hearing this immediately sink back, *do you hear?!* and from this point on he doesn't even try to hide his disapproval of them, so that they pretend to be listening with all their might, as they hear that *Odysseus he did not find within; for he sat weeping on the shore, where, as of old, with tears and groans and griefs racking his heart, he watched the barren sea and poured forth tears. And now Calypso, the heavenly goddess, questioned Hermes, seating him on a handsome, shining chair: "Pray, Hermes of the golden wand, why are you come, honored and welcome though you are?* tamtamtamtararam, tamtamtamtam, the old man keeps shaking his index finger past some lines, searching again for a place in the text, oh yes, here it is, *So saying, the goddess laid a table, loading it with ambrosia and mixing ruddy nectar; and so the guide, the Giant-killer, drank and ate. But when the meal was ended and his heart was stayed with food, then thus he answered her and said: "Goddess, you question me, a god, about my coming hither, and I will truly tell my story as you bid . . . a man is with you, the most unfortunate of all who fought for Priam's town nine years and in the tenth destroyed the city and departed home. They on their homeward way offended*

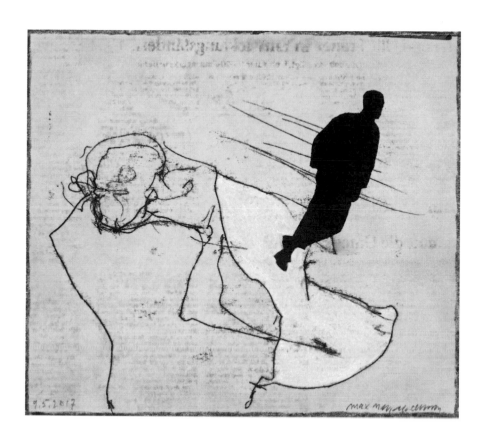

*Athena, who raised ill winds against them and a heavy
sea. Thus all the rest of his good comrades perished,
but the wind and water brought him here. This is the
man Zeus now bids you send away, and quickly too, for
it is not ordained that he shall perish far from friends;
it is his lot to see his friends once more and reach his
high-roofed house and native land." As he said this,
Calypso, the heavenly goddess, shuddered,* and by now
the two Japanese are clutching each other's hands and
shrinking back on their chairs as far as they can, because
the old man once again is raising his finger on high and
repeating, *Calypso, the heavenly goddess,* but now at a
volume so loud that even the customers slouching at the
bar look his way, but he just keeps reciting in the same
loud voice that promises precious little good in store for
the two Japanese tourists, *Hard-hearted are you gods
and envious beyond all to grudge that goddesses should
mate with men and take without disguise mortals for
lovers ... now you gods grudge me the mortal tarrying
here. Yet it was I who saved him, as he rode astride his
keel alone, when Zeus with a gleaming bolt smote his
swift ship and wrecked it in the middle of the wine-dark
sea. There all the rest of his good comrades perished,
but the wind and water brought him here. I loved and
cherished him, and often said that I would make him
an immortal, young forever. But since the will of aegis-
bearing Zeus no god may cross or set at naught, let him
depart, if Zeus commands and bids it, over the barren
sea! Only I will not aid him on his way, for I have no
ships fitted with oars, nor crews to bear him over the
broad ocean-ridges ... Then said to her the guide, the
Giant-killer,* tamtaratamtam, tamtamtam, raratamtam,
once again that index finger is looking for something,

and finds it, *the potent nymph hastened to brave Odysseus, obedient to the words of Zeus. She found him sitting on the shore, and from his eyes the tears were never dried; his sweet life ebbed away in longings for his home, because the nymph pleased him no more,* and then the old man booms at them, *huhh,* startling the couple, who look at him as if he's a madman and now they really have to escape, while he, eyes ablaze, exulting at each dactyl and spondee, just keeps on going, *being compelled, he slept at night within the hollow grotto as she desired, not he. But in the daytime, sitting on the rocks and sands, with tears and groans and griefs racking his heart, he watched the barren sea and poured forth tears. Now drawing near, the heavenly goddess said: "Unhappy man, sorrow no longer here, nor let your days be wasted, for I at last will freely let you go,"* and with that he lowers his book to give the couple a long and reproachful look, or maybe by now not even reproachful, but rather resigned to the inevitable, to the futility of representing a hapless superiority, a look full of the melancholy of goodwill misunderstood and frustrated, so that all he can say, in a voice cracking with emotion, is, *Do you realize that Calypso, she was a death-nymph?!* Whereupon the Japanese couple respond with the slightest shake of their heads, and *Do you know,* the old man raises his broken voice again, *what an island of the dead is?!* No, the two Japanese again shake their heads, and the old man, his hand grown lethargic but still holding the book in his lap, says, *I will pay the cost of the trip there and back,* but even he's aware that the Japanese are not going to respond to this either, they merely sit there, petrified, obviously hoping for a way out, and the tourist guide just gazes at them, without saying anything, shaking his head, baffled, he cannot fathom this, he simply cannot make out why people reject what's best for them, and that's what's been transpiring for some time at the neighboring table, but I'm no longer paying attention, busy taking in the faces at the bar, and my eyes turn for an instant to that peculiar party again, the exhausted and resigned tourist guide whose eyes have still not left his Japanese couple even as they're clearly contemplating the shortest route to the exit, encouraging each other with mute nods to go first, but by now I've lost all interest and, paying them no mind, am content to clasp my empty mug (I finished my coffee a while ago) until suddenly my ears perk up when, as he's snapping the book shut and slipping it back in his pocket with a theatrical gesture, the old guide utters a phrase, he's saying something to the terrified couple that sounds like "the island is unsettled"—at this I look up suddenly, had I heard correctly, and I had, because the old man, as if this is his final pitch, beyond which he can do no more, repeats it several times—"the island is unsettled"—and with that, considering the conversation over, the old guide springs up from the table without sparing another glance at the totally bewildered and befuddled Japanese couple, and storms out, declaring to the bartender on the way, "The right to hospitality is finished, tourism is dead!" and he slams out of the bar in high dudgeon, and with that the whole scene ends for me as well, it's over, and the world around me stops too, because all I can hear inside my head is "unsettled," I repeat this to myself a few times, I keep pushing the word forward in time a little bit, I keep turning it round and round until there's nothing left to turn, and only the question remains, could this be possible? could it be that, beyond the fact that I've found my way here and, as my intuition tells me, in all probability thrown them off my tracks, is there now something else that surpasses even this probability? that perhaps there's another place in the vicinity even more extraordinary than this one, a place that's uninhabited?! could that be possible? that it's then all over? that I've escaped? or at least, that I've managed to postpone the inevitable? because if that other place— and obviously that too has to be an island, this certainty flashes feverishly in my head—is in fact uninhabited, and if the ferry traffic in the off-season is as sparse as the old man had been claiming, then it could be an almost safe terrain for me to survive, to survive at least for another season, and who knows, perhaps this means that I can be master of my own fate, that they'll lose track of me for good—can I muster enough belief? I turn to the side for a better view of the old guide, not to hear his words but to see his eyes, to judge whether I can believe that the island he's been here recommending so enthusiastically to the unlucky couple could really be a refuge for me. And—even though they're no longer present, no longer in my vicinity—I find those old eyes very much to my liking.

16. Good, but not good enough

I'll soon leave the little port behind, so small it barely deserves to be called a port, all it has is one rickety landing stage and a few buoys where small, usually overloaded light boats stop briefly, but this time with only five passengers aboard, including myself, and the others, judging by their characteristic outfits, are all Japanese tourists—here to see in the course of four hours the island's "miraculous natural wonders," and, if they're still curious enough, take in the villages that survive mainly thanks to tourism, and because of "Odysseus himself," as the young man piloting the small boat puts it in his broken English—and the Japanese, I realize, clearly can have nothing to do with my saga, moreover the couple seen earlier isn't among them, so I barely feel any necessity of casting any special sideways glances to look them over, though I do nonetheless, and they pass inspection, they're certainly Japanese and clearly harmless tourists—so I disembark from the boat with a feeling almost of liberation, and I set out toward the interior of the island, walking with the others for the time being, the usual intuitive tactic, to follow, to remain alongside them for a while, not exactly with them (I have no intentions of engaging in conversation, but I'm not exactly keeping apart, either, so for a while we advance on a well-marked path more or less as one group until we arrive at a tranquil small pond, from which another lake, a larger one, opens up, in the far end of which—according to the guide map on a pole beside the landing stage—

lies a diminutive little island with a ruined monastery named Crkva Sv. Marije, after the chapel once upon a time consecrated to the Virgin Mary, and here the four tourists immediately park themselves, and with oohs and ahs proceed to admire the view of the lake, while I casually move on, as one who came here for something else, not for the lake and not for Crkva Sv. Marije, but— and this wouldn't be unusual at a wildlife sanctuary—for the sake of a rare butterfly, for example, or to study the winter habitat of some special plant, it makes no difference, the other four, if they want, could certainly imagine some reason, some completely obvious explanation for my not remaining with them, and anyway they clearly forget all about me within minutes, gazing upon the lake and almost immediately starting to take photos of each other, directing expectant looks into the distance across the calm surface of the water, while I—after a few minutes, for I'm not speeding up my pace—disappear from view and soon find myself in some thickets, without as yet going far from the lakeshore, though after a while, when I take a turn away from the lake, plunging into an even denser part of the woods that cover the whole island, I can see that the others—now a thousand or so feet below me—are still on the same spot, waiting for the small motor launch that will transport them across the lake all the way to the Crkva Sv. Marije—and the woods are very thick where I find myself now, and what I first become conscious of among the Aleppo pines is me myself, how I'm not falling back on my usual tempo—that not too fast, not too slow, but at times slow, at times fast, racing, throbbing pace—no, I'm advancing now at the same even tempo I'd just used to put some distance between me and the others, there's no reason to rush at

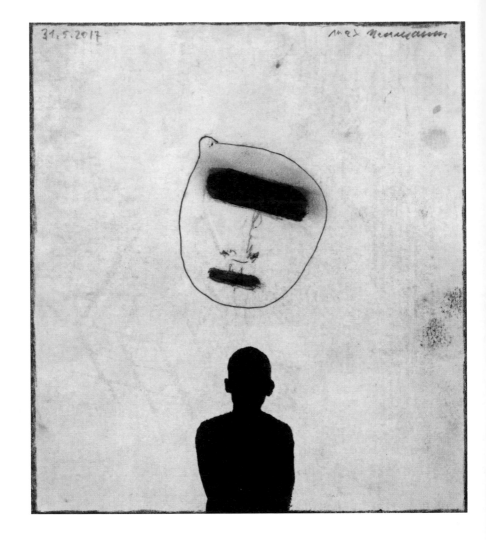

all, although the thought that I might be mistaken gives me the shivers, and then the thought that maybe I'm not mistaken also gives me the shivers, or, more precisely, the thought *why this sudden calm* gives me the shivers, but then I give in to it, true, only after attempting to discover what might have gone wrong, trying to come up with reasons why this tranquility, a tranquility that I haven't felt since being compelled to be on the run, is in fact a mental derangement, but I soon stop speculating and decide that the calm must be caused by simple exhaustion, so I keep up my measured pace, realizing that my body, that my entire organism is indisposed for anything except tranquility, and now I think, very well, if that's what my body wants, so be it, and that's the moment when I start to believe, even if with certain misgivings, that it is the island itself imposing this calm, the island that's perhaps not just here to conceal me from danger but could possibly prove to be my downright savior, and I can feel myself being gradually liberated from the crushing pressure, as if, after existing under a bell weighing a thousand tons, that bell of a thousand tons is being slowly lifted, and the fresh air is streaming in, and I can breathe again, I can inhale deeply, I haven't been able to breathe for decades, or at least for years, months, weeks now, and I advance further into the woods until I come across a well-worn path that leads me to a tiny village named Polace where the only person I encounter is a postcard vendor who's sound asleep, his head resting on his folded arms, and even his dog-eared postcards, faded leftovers of the summer season, are sound asleep as well, along with a few bundles of parsley bound with delicate grape tendrils, and I cut across Polace without a single soul being aware that I've been there, and I see the road ahead, flanked by the dark tranquility of the Aleppo pines, with an increasing sense of liberation, I don't know where they're leading me, but it's good the way it is, by now I can say that it's good, and for the first time, yes from here on, this goodness is not a trap but ... just good, for it's indeed good that fate has cast me up here, and it's good that Mljet is able to make me believe in this, and it's good that I know how to believe in something again, in a word, good, good, good, I keep repeating, as I walk on by the side of the road, walking and walking, and repeating that it's good, but I go on, because yes, it's good, but not yet good enough.

17. Toward hope

 My feet are now so light that it feels as if I'm not even really walking, just slashing straight ahead, and even as darkness falls, I keep marching on through the whole night, and the next day I keep it up, and when evening comes again, instead of being tired, I feel more and more rested, my feet are still so light, and my march keeps on as before, advancing unfettered down my road on this unknown, uninhabited island where I'm being driven by a power I've never known before, what's more, a power whose very existence I'd doubted until now, and even now I don't know what this is, I don't know what to call it, but I don't mind at all that there aren't any words for it, all the better, it simply *is*, and in fact now that I'm completely certain that I've left the assassins behind and that this road with its Aleppo pines is leading me to a place where they'll never find me, where I won't have anything at all to fear, as long as I keep going, going, going ever onward, on this island that obviously has no end, and never will have an end, where my light feet just keep going and going.

18. At Calypso's

The sign indicates that Blato's to the right, but I have no intention to go to Blato, I don't want to go anywhere, I want to abide where I am, on this road, because all I want is to keep moving forward, enjoying how light my feet feel, as light as a feather, everything, my entire body's as light as a feather, in fact I could even say—if there were anyone to say it to—that there's really nothing for my feet to carry, because my whole body's turned into a handful of feathers, my body has no weight whatsoever, weight's vanished from my life, and everything around me is weightless, nothing but weightless pines, nothing but ever-weightless Ragusan centaurea and Juban spurge to the left and right, wherever I turn my head, and the earth I'm treading on has no weight either, and the sky, this once again resplendently blue sky, now curving overhead, is a single feather, and the Bora's gone now without a trace, whatever wind remains is just a breeze, keeping everything afloat, me on my feet, the earth underfoot, the sky overhead, as well as the trees, and the silent sea crows that perch floating on the branches, but also each and every blade of grass, so that everything in existence is floating, and now evening's falling again, how many days has it been since I disembarked from that small boat on the island's west side, the light's diminishing and receding, tinting the sky behind my back, but I'm not turning around to look, I'm not beholding the horizon, and for that matter I've seen hardly anything except at Babino Polje when I notice a sign leaning to one side declaring

which comes at an opportune moment, just as I'm thinking that it's about time to take a turn to the right, and
just as I'm thinking that, it's possible to turn there, onto
a meager, winding little path presenting itself to me like
a gift, and I now begin a steep descent, setting out on
it, this twisting, narrow little path sloping down at a
very steep angle, flanked by tall bushes, and in the distance only alders everywhere—no pines or centaurea
or spurge—suddenly it's alders, horned owls and hawks
squatting on their branches, all this I can see at a glance,
but who cares about the sudden change in the trees, or
about those peculiar, motionless birds on the branches,
only the path flanked by dense bushes counts, yes,
there's just enough room, barely, and the downslope's
so steep that not only is my body weightless, now as the
descent gathers momentum, there's less and less control over my footing, yes, I'm practically flying, faster
and faster downhill, one sharp turn follows another, I
can't see what lies ahead, these hairpin turns and bushes
hides what lies ahead, but one more sharp turn and I
suddenly see the sea—and the sea's tremendous, it's tre-
mendously blue, spread out there to my right, way down
below, it's engulfing everything that can be engulfed,
and I'm seeing it, I'm keeping my eyes on it and I'm flying
downhill, I see it and my heart's bursting with joy, because I lived to see *this*—my feet no longer have to carry
me, I'm soaring downhill swift as the wind, barely taking those curves, until suddenly—around a bend, leaping
up at me from the left—I see a gigantic, broad-funneled,
profoundly deep abyss, its eroding edge partitioned
from the path by a few meters of wire fence attached to

31.5.2017

dilapidated wooden stakes leaning every which way, no barrier to anyone crashing into it, no barrier for me I'm thinking, at the last moment, or rather at the end of the last moment given to me there, with the ground so loose, at the edge of the precipice, so loose and crumbly that it's a miracle that the fence posts still stand somehow at all, even if incapable of restraining, forcing to recoil, or catching anyone who, such as me, bursts with explosive speed around the turn, slams into it, no, there's nothing else to do but break through the fence and tumble into this deepest of chasms, and I was not able to know that down there below at the bottom of the rocky cliff a grotto opened, *a cave which was accessible only from the sea, it has no other egress except underwater, meaning swimming through an opening under the sea, which is exactly what a group of scuba divers is doing at just about the same time, emerging from the water filling the bottom of the cave and raising their eyes to the far-off heights up above, where they see up there, high up there, hanging over the edge of the precipice, a couple of rotting fence posts, only held back from tumbling into the depths by a few wires—there a moment earlier they might have seen something smash through the fence, perhaps something dying of fright in midair—but they didn't see anything except the dangling posts, because that was over, that was all over, though there they are, five scuba divers, two women and three men, and one after another they popped up out of the water at the lip of the cave's mouth, exultantly, perhaps because they'd succeeded in finding what they'd been looking for, yes, they'd made it, they're here, and, outshouting the crash of the waves against the grotto's rocky wall, one of the women, managing to free herself from her diving mask and spitting out the mouthpiece, started leaping about triumphantly, stabbing her fists skyward, yelling* Ha-lloo, Ha-lloo, Calypso, we're here, Ha-lloo, *and the others, similarly electrified, start jubilantly splashing the water around in the echoing cave, and then slowly, one after another, they lift themselves up and with awkward shuffling of their flippered feet trudge along the lip of the grotto and, all staring upward, amazed, raise their gaze meter by meter higher and higher up the wall, up to the broken semicircle of the precipice's upper rim at an enormous height above, when the oldest among them, a man with a ponytail down his back, possibly their guide, notices something on a dry strip of beach to the right of the mouth of the cave, and their gazing eyes suddenly lower and cloud over as they try to make out what it is their companion's discovered, but no one else makes a move, only he, the oldest one, sets out to check what it is, approaching it cautiously, for that thing might have been anything, and after reaching it, and giving it a kick or two, he waves to the others, calling:* "It's all right, just a dead rat, nothing to worry about."

19. No

 No, I was never giving up.

The music is available at the links below, as well as through the QR codes at the beginning of each chapter

www.ndbooks.com/chasing-homer/00
www.ndbooks.com/chasing-homer/01
www.ndbooks.com/chasing-homer/02
www.ndbooks.com/chasing-homer/03
www.ndbooks.com/chasing-homer/04
www.ndbooks.com/chasing-homer/05
www.ndbooks.com/chasing-homer/06
www.ndbooks.com/chasing-homer/07
www.ndbooks.com/chasing-homer/08
www.ndbooks.com/chasing-homer/09
www.ndbooks.com/chasing-homer/10
www.ndbooks.com/chasing-homer/11
www.ndbooks.com/chasing-homer/12
www.ndbooks.com/chasing-homer/13
www.ndbooks.com/chasing-homer/14
www.ndbooks.com/chasing-homer/15
www.ndbooks.com/chasing-homer/16
www.ndbooks.com/chasing-homer/17
www.ndbooks.com/chasing-homer/18
www.ndbooks.com/chasing-homer/19